Also by Calvin Garner

Echoes Of The Hunted: The Hearts of Men
Silent Flames: Office Temptations Revealed
Wordless Whispers: A Tale of Subdued Longings
Agent Ryder: A Soldier's Plight
Deadly Skies: Murder In The clouds
The Algorithm Of Ambition
The Quantum Classroom
The Pulse Of Eternity
Allied Thrones: The Last Pact

Allied Thrones
The Last Pact

Author:
Calvin Garner

Copyright © 2024
By Calvin Garner
All rights reserved.

NO PART OF THIS BOOK may be reproduced or transmitted in any form or by any means, electronic or mechanical, including but not limited to photocopying, recording, or by any information storage and retrieval system, without permission in writing from the publisher. This copyright notice asserts the author's ownership of this Book and specifies that no part of the book may be reproduced without permission from the publisher.

Table On Contents

Prologue
Chapter 1

The Gathering Storm

Chapter 2

The Warrior's Dilemma

Chapter 3

Secrets of the Sorceress

Chapter 4

Diplomatic Games

Chapter 5

The Young Heir's Burden

Chapter 6

Shadows of Nocturne

Chapter 7

The Council of Kings

Chapter 8

Betrayal in the Ranks

Chapter 9

The Rising Tide

Chapter 10

Bonds of War

Chapter 11

The Prophecy Unfolds

Chapter 12

Allies and Adversaries

Chapter 13

The Battle for Unity

Chapter 14

The Price of Peace

Chapter 15

A New Dawn

Prologue

In the beginning, when the sun had begun its slow descent and shadows stretched long over the land, the sky darkened with a fearsome omen. Legends spoke of a time when the heavens would be rent asunder, and the kingdoms would face a foe from beyond the stars. The heavens grew heavy, thunder rumbling as if the gods themselves were angry. The stars, once bright and welcoming, flickered like dying embers. Dark clouds, thick and foreboding, gathered in the sky, obscuring the sun's once-golden light. Across the land, whispers spread like wildfire. The five kingdoms, each proud and mighty in their own right, felt a chill seep into their bones. Elders in their stone towers and priests in their sacred temples looked to the heavens, their faces pale and drawn. They spoke of a prophecy, an ancient promise made long ago that spoke of a day when all would fall into shadow unless they came together.

From the cold north of Valdor to the warm southern seas of Eryndor, each ruler, each leader, saw the darkening sky and felt a growing dread. Their hearts pounded like war drums, for this was no mere storm. This was the harbinger of an age-old threat, one that had slumbered in the dark corners of the world, waiting for its time to strike. The people, too, were uneasy, their usual laughter replaced with worried murmurs as they looked to their leaders for answers.

In the midst of this, the ancient scrolls, hidden away for centuries, were unearthed, revealing words that seemed to glow with a light of their own. The prophecy had awoken, and with it, the destiny of all the kingdoms was set to change forever.

Chapter 1

The Gathering Storm

In the days when the world was young, and the sky was clear and untroubled, the heavens grew heavy with a dark promise. The sun, once a golden chariot that rode high and warm, began to falter in its course. Clouds of deepest gray, dark as the shadowed abyss, spread like ink spilled upon the canvas of the sky. Thunder roared like a beast awakened from slumber, shaking the very bones of the earth. Lightning danced across the firmament, casting jagged scars upon the darkened dome.

The elders spoke in hushed tones, their voices trembling like leaves in a storm. They knew the old stories well, tales passed from generation to generation, whispering of a time when the world would be shrouded in darkness. Those stories spoke of a prophecy, one that had been written in ancient runes on scrolls lost to the sands of time. The skies themselves seemed to echo those old fears, darkening with an unnatural haste.

From the frozen heights of Valdor, where the snow-capped peaks scraped the heavens, to the lush, green valleys of Eryndor, where the sea whispered secrets to the shore, the signs were clear. Kings and queens, each ruler in their grand halls of power, looked up and saw the same grim sight. The once-predictable rhythms of nature were thrown into disarray. Crops began to wither, rivers ran low, and animals grew restless. The land itself seemed to sense the coming calamity.

The old scrolls, buried deep in the vaults of forgotten libraries, spoke of an age-old enemy that had slumbered in the dark corners of the world. The prophecy told of a time when this dark force would awaken, driven by a hunger to consume all light and life. The very stars, which had long been the guiding lights for travelers and dreamers alike, flickered like dying embers. Each flicker was a whisper of the impending doom, a cold warning carried on the wind.

In the royal courts, rulers held fast to their thrones with shaking hands, their faces as pale as the moon. Each kingdom had its own fears and hopes, but the darkening sky made it clear that the threat was one and the same. Councils were called, messengers were sent, and the air buzzed with tension. The great halls that once rang with laughter and the clinking of goblets now echoed with solemn discussions and frantic plans.

From the land of Valdor, where the warriors' hearts beat with the rhythm of battle, came a leader who could not ignore the darkening sky. He was a warrior of great renown, known for his courage and strength. Yet even he felt a shiver as the skies grew black. The thought of facing an unknown enemy was enough to make the bravest of souls hesitate.

Far to the south, in the warm, sunlit lands of Eryndor, the sea itself seemed troubled. Fishermen spoke of strange tides and fish that leapt from the water in terror. The ocean, once a source of life and bounty, seemed to warn of the danger that loomed on the horizon. The prince, who had always been a master of the seas, now looked out at the darkening waves with a heart heavy with dread.

In the mountain realm of Tharic, where the air was crisp and the land rich with resources, the young heir faced his own trials. He was not yet seasoned in the ways of leadership, and the darkening sky added to his burdens. The weight of his ancestors' expectations bore down upon him. He knew that the coming storm would test not only his resolve but also the strength of his people.

The Sorceress Queen of Aelarion, wise and enigmatic, felt the shift in the magic that flowed through her land. Her kingdom was renowned for its mystical arts, but even her powers could not penetrate the gloom that had settled over the world. The scrolls she had studied as a child spoke of such times, but seeing it unfold was another matter entirely. Her heart ached with the knowledge that her kingdom would not remain untouched by this growing threat.

From the shadowy realm of Nocturne, the enigmatic Shadow Prince watched with an inscrutable gaze. His land, hidden in perpetual twilight, had always harbored secrets. The darkening sky was but a mirror to the darkness within. He knew the ancient legends, but now they seemed more than just tales. They were a call to action, a signal that the time of reckoning was near.

As the darkened sky continued its relentless advance, the rulers of the five kingdoms knew they had to act. The old prophecy, once thought to be a distant fear, was now a looming reality. The scrolls had been found, and their words, once dismissed as mere stories, were now a guide for the uncertain times ahead. The prophecy spoke of an alliance forged in the fires of adversity, of kingdoms coming together to face the encroaching darkness.

The people, too, felt the weight of the prophecy. Their laughter had faded, replaced by worried murmurs and uneasy glances. The darkening sky had become a symbol of the trials they would face. Every village, every town, had its own stories of fear and hope, woven into the fabric of their daily lives. The old legends were not just tales of old; they were becoming the reality of their present.

The sky continued to darken, a constant reminder of the danger that loomed. The stars, once bright and full of promise, were now hidden behind the oppressive clouds. The winds carried whispers of the coming storm, and the earth trembled as if it, too, could sense the approaching darkness. The prophecy was no longer a distant fear but a pressing reality that demanded action.

As the heavens darkened and the earth prepared for the trials ahead, the rulers and their people braced themselves. They knew that the coming days would test their strength, their unity, and their resolve. The darkening sky was not just a sign of what was to come but a challenge to be met with courage and determination. The ancient prophecy had awakened, and with it, the destiny of the five kingdoms was set upon a new path.

Chapter 2

The Warrior's Dilemma

In the rugged highlands of Valdor, where the wind howls through ancient pines and the mountains pierce the sky, the Warrior King sat brooding in his great hall. His name was Thorne, a man whose sword had sung many a battle hymn and whose name was known across the lands. The air in the hall was thick with smoke from the hearths, and the flickering torchlight painted shadows on the stone walls, making them seem like giants in the dark.

King Thorne, a figure of imposing strength and battle-worn wisdom, looked out across the land he had fought so hard to defend. His eyes, sharp as an eagle's, were troubled. The darkening sky was more than just a sign of a storm, it was a herald of something far more ominous. The old stories spoke of a prophecy, and though he had heard such tales before, never had they felt so real, so near.

His council gathered around him, each one a warrior or advisor, their faces a mix of worry and determination. The clinking of their armor and the rustle of their cloaks were the only sounds breaking the silence, save for the occasional crackle of the fire. Thorne's trusted general, a burly man with a beard like a wild bramble, spoke first. "My king, the darkening sky and the whispers of the old prophecy unsettle us all. What must we do?"

Thorne's hand clenched around the hilt of his sword, the blade resting on the floor beside his throne. His mind wrestled with the weight of leadership. Valdor had always stood alone, proud and fierce, a fortress against the world's many threats. To unite with other kingdoms, once enemies, felt like a betrayal of everything he had fought for.

The general continued, "We cannot face this darkness alone. The stories say that the threat is beyond anything we have ever seen. The other kingdoms must be brought to our side."

Thorne's brow furrowed, his thoughts a storm of conflicting loyalties. The idea of negotiating peace with those he had once fought against seemed like madness. In the past, he had led his people with the sword and the shield, but now the path before him was less clear. Could he trust these former foes? Could they even hope to unite against a threat they barely understood?

Among the council was a young squire, eager and bright-eyed, who had grown up hearing tales of Valdor's might. He stepped forward, his voice trembling but full of earnestness. "My lord, the other kingdoms have their own strengths. Together, we could be stronger. I've heard that the sorceress of Aelarion commands great magic, and the Prince of Eryndor has a fleet that rules the seas. Imagine what we could achieve if we joined forces."

Thorne's gaze softened for a moment as he looked at the squire, remembering his own youth and the dreams that had once seemed so clear. But reality had a way of clouding those dreams with shadows. He sighed deeply, the weight of his position pressing heavily on him. His mind turned to the old scrolls, their worn edges and faded ink, filled with prophecies of doom and salvation. He had always dismissed them as mere tales, but now they seemed to speak with a more urgent voice.

"Would you have us put our faith in tales?" Thorne's voice was rough, like gravel underfoot. "What if these allies are merely seeking to take advantage of our plight?"

The general nodded, understanding the king's hesitation. "It is a risk, but what choice do we have? The darkening sky and the ancient prophecy make it clear that we face a threat unlike any other. We must at least try to seek an alliance."

The room fell silent again, the air heavy with unspoken fears and hopes. Thorne's heart was heavy, torn between his duty to his people and the uncertain promise of unity with old rivals. His mind wandered to the many battles he had fought, the bloodshed and sacrifice, and he wondered if this new battle required something different—a different kind of courage.

Outside the hall, the wind howled louder, as if urging him to make a decision. Thorne stood, his figure tall and imposing against the flickering light. His eyes, once fierce and unyielding, now held a hint of weariness. He had always fought with the blade, but now he faced a battle of the mind and heart. The weight of leadership was not only in the battles fought but, in the decisions, made in times of uncertainty.

He turned to his council, his voice steady despite the turmoil within. "Prepare emissaries. We will reach out to the other kingdoms and seek their counsel. I will not promise them our allegiance, but I will hear what they have to say. We must be wise in our choices."

The general and the others nodded, their faces reflecting a mixture of relief and apprehension. Thorne knew that this was only the beginning of a long and uncertain journey. The darkening sky was a reminder of the unknown challenges ahead, and the prophecy, once a distant tale, was now a reality that demanded action.

As the council dispersed and the hall grew quiet, Thorne stood alone, staring out at the stormy night. The heavens roared and lightning flashed, casting brief illuminations on the land below. The warrior king felt the burden of his role more keenly than ever. The path ahead was shrouded in darkness, but he knew that he could not face it alone. The future of Valdor, and perhaps all the kingdoms, lay in the decisions he would make in the days to come.

Chapter 3

Secrets of the Sorceress

In the heart of Aelarion, where ancient trees whispered secrets and mystical creatures danced in the moonlight, the Sorceress Queen Elara sat in her grand chamber. The room was filled with a soft, emerald glow from enchanted lanterns that floated like fireflies in the dimness. Shelves lined with ancient tomes and artifacts filled every corner, their dusty covers and worn spines holding the secrets of ages past.

Elara, cloaked in a robe of deep blue and silver, her hair cascading like a river of stars, moved with a grace that was both captivating and eerie. She had seen many winters and many cycles of the moon, but never had the world seemed so fraught with danger. Her eyes, bright and piercing, gazed upon a large, ancient scroll that lay open upon an old oak table. The scroll was covered in runes and symbols, their meanings long known only to the sorceress. The scroll told of a prophecy, an old tale of darkness and unity that had been hidden away for centuries. Elara had always believed in the power of the prophecy but had kept its details shrouded in mystery. The darkening sky, a portent that had come true, stirred something deep within her, something that made the old stories feel more urgent and real.

As Elara pondered the ancient text, a soft knock came upon the chamber door. Her trusted advisor, a wise old man with a beard as white as the winter snow, entered. His eyes were shadowed with worry. "My queen, the sky grows darker with each passing night. The other kingdoms are stirring, and the people of Aelarion are filled with unease. What do the scrolls say of this time?"

Elara looked up, her expression a mask of calm determination. "The scrolls speak of a darkness that can only be faced by the combined strength of all the kingdoms. The prophecy is clear—only by uniting can we stand against the encroaching shadow."

Her advisor, with a furrowed brow, took a step closer. "But the prophecy also speaks of betrayal, of treachery among allies. How can we trust that the other kingdoms will truly stand with us?"

Elara's gaze hardened. "That is the danger we face. The prophecy warns us that even as we seek unity, we must be wary of those who might seek to undermine it. It is not simply enough to come together; we must also be vigilant."

The chamber fell silent except for the distant murmur of the wind outside, carrying the eerie whispers of the ancient woods. Elara walked to a large, ornate mirror, its surface shimmering with a light of its own. She placed her hand upon it, and images began to form—visions of distant lands and people, of battles and alliances. The mirror showed her the Warrior King of Valdor, standing tall and resolute but clearly troubled. Next, it revealed the young Prince of Eryndor, his face lined with concern as he gazed out over the turbulent sea. The images shifted to the mountain realm of Tharic and then to the shadowy realm of Nocturne, where a dark figure watched with inscrutable eyes.

Elara turned back to her advisor, her face set in a serious expression. "The other kingdoms have their own fears and uncertainties. Each one must be approached with care and caution. We must send emissaries to speak with them, but we must also be prepared for the possibility that some may have hidden agendas."

Her advisor nodded. "And what of the dark force that threatens us? What more do the scrolls say of this enemy?"

Elara's eyes darkened as she thought of the ancient foe. "The scrolls tell of a shadow that seeks to consume all light and life. It is a force of great power, one that has waited for centuries in the dark corners of the world. It is said that this shadow feeds on fear and division. Our greatest strength lies in our unity, but if we falter, we may become easy prey for this darkness."

As the night wore on, Elara continued to study the scrolls, her mind racing with the possibilities and dangers ahead. She knew that the fate of Aelarion, and indeed all the kingdoms, rested on the balance of their actions and decisions. Trust and betrayal were two sides of the same coin, and the challenge was to forge alliances while guarding against deceit.

In the dim light of her chamber, Elara's thoughts turned to the ancient magic that flowed through Aelarion. The magic was strong and ancient, a gift from the land itself. Yet, as powerful as it was, it could not stand alone against the growing darkness. The prophecy spoke of a time when all magic, all strength, would need to be combined to face the coming storm.

Elara knew that the time had come to act. She must call upon her allies, even those she had once considered rivals. The emissaries needed to be chosen with care, those who would represent Aelarion with honor and wisdom. She had to ensure that the message was clear—that unity was the only path to survival. The future of all the kingdoms hung in the balance, and every choice made in the coming days would shape the world to come.

As dawn approached, the first light of day began to seep into the chamber, casting a soft glow over the ancient scrolls and enchanted artifacts. Elara's resolve was set. The time for secrets was over. The prophecies had awakened, and now the true test of strength and unity would begin. The shadows on the horizon were not just a threat but a challenge that would require the combined efforts of all the kingdoms to overcome. The Sorceress Queen was ready to meet that challenge, armed with the knowledge of the past and the courage to face the future.

Chapter 4

Diplomatic Games

In the grand halls of Eryndor, where the air was thick with the scent of salt and the murmur of the sea, the Prince Eldric faced a challenge unlike any he had known. His land was a kingdom of ships and tides, where the waves were his allies and the winds his messengers. Yet, as the darkening sky threatened, the prince found himself in the midst of a tempest of another sort, a storm of politics and alliances. The palace was abuzz with activity as emissaries from the other kingdoms arrived. Each one brought with them their own aura of power and intrigue, their cloaks and banners marking their lands. Eldric's advisors, wise and experienced, buzzed around him, their voices a cacophony of strategy and concern.

Eldric stood by the grand window overlooking the bustling harbor, his eyes scanning the arrival of ships. The sea was restless, mirroring the turmoil within the palace. His trusted advisor, a shrewd old man with a keen mind for negotiations, approached with a furrowed brow. "My prince, the emissaries are here. They come with their own agendas and expectations. We must be careful."

The prince nodded, his face a mask of calm determination. "What do we know of these visitors? What are their true intentions?"

The advisor's gaze turned thoughtful. "The emissary from Valdor is a seasoned warrior, known for his fierce pride and strong sense of duty. He will likely be wary of any suggestion that might seem to undermine his kingdom's strength. The sorceress of Aelarion, on the other hand, is a mystery. Her motives are shrouded in secrecy, and her presence here might be more than it seems."

Eldric's eyes narrowed as he considered this. The threat from the darkening sky had made it clear that old rivalries needed to be set aside, but mistrust still lingered like a shadow. He knew that forging an alliance would not be easy. Each kingdom had its own fears and ambitions, and the path to unity would be fraught with challenges.

The first to meet with Eldric was the emissary from Valdor, a burly man with a beard like tangled brambles and a voice that boomed like a war horn. His presence commanded respect, and his every gesture spoke of a warrior's discipline. Eldric welcomed him with the courtesy due his rank, but the conversation was guarded, each word weighed with caution.

"We face a grave threat," Eldric began, his voice steady. "The darkening sky is not just a sign of storms but of a greater danger. We must discuss how our kingdoms can unite against this threat."

The emissary from Valdor nodded solemnly but said little. His eyes, sharp and watchful, assessed Eldric's every move. "Valdor has always fought for its own survival. We do not easily trust outsiders, but the signs are clear. We must consider how to align our forces."

Next came the emissary from Aelarion, a graceful figure cloaked in a shimmering robe that seemed to change colors in the light. Her presence was captivating, but Eldric could not shake the feeling that there was more to her than met the eye. She spoke with a voice that flowed like a river, her words both enchanting and enigmatic.

"The magic of Aelarion is ancient and powerful," she said. "But even our strength may not be enough against the encroaching shadow. We seek not only to join forces but to understand the depths of this threat. What have you learned of its nature?"

Eldric's gaze was steady. "We have seen signs of its power, but the true extent remains unknown. We must share what we know and find a way to combine our strengths."

The discussions continued over the days, each meeting a dance of diplomacy and subtlety. The emissaries from Tharic and Nocturne added their voices to the chorus of negotiations. The emissary from Tharic, a young man with a sharp wit and a strategic mind, sought assurances that his kingdom's resources would be valued. The envoy from Nocturne, dark and enigmatic, spoke little but watched the proceedings with intense interest.

In the grand hall, the debates grew heated as each representative argued for their kingdom's interests. The air crackled with tension, the light from the chandeliers casting long shadows on the walls. Eldric's role was to mediate, to find common ground amid the clashing interests. His mind raced as he weighed each proposal, each concern, striving to keep the focus on the greater threat that bound them all.

One evening, as the sun set and the sky turned a deep crimson, Eldric gathered the emissaries for a final meeting. The discussions had been long and arduous, and progress was slow. Yet, the prince sensed that the time had come to press for a resolution.

"My friends," Eldric began, his voice carrying a note of earnestness, "the darkening sky grows ever darker, and time is not on our side. We must decide how to act, not just as individual kingdoms but as a united force. Each of us has something to offer, and together we can forge a path through this darkness."

The emissaries exchanged glances, their faces reflecting the weight of the decision before them. The emissary from Valdor spoke first, his voice gruff but resolved. "We are warriors, and we will stand with those who fight beside us. We must have clear terms and mutual respect if this alliance is to hold."

The sorceress from Aelarion nodded in agreement. "The magic of Aelarion will be at your disposal, but we must trust one another. The shadows we face are treacherous, and we cannot afford to falter."

As the meetings drew to a close, an agreement began to take shape. The kingdoms would form a united front, each contributing their unique strengths—Valdor's military might, Aelarion's magic, Eryndor's naval power, Tharic's resources, and Nocturne's shadowy intelligence. Yet, the path forward was not without its hurdles. The emissaries' words had been chosen carefully, their promises weighed with the knowledge that old rivalries die hard.

The grand hall of Eryndor, once a place of contention, now buzzed with a tentative hope. Eldric knew that forging this alliance was only the first step. The true test would be in the unity of action and the strength of their combined forces. The darkening sky loomed ever closer, and the diplomatic games, though critical, were just the beginning of the trials ahead.

Chapter 5

The Young Heir's Burden

In the land of Tharic, where the mountains stood like ancient guardians and the forests whispered secrets to those who would listen, young Prince Aric faced a burden heavier than any crown. The kingdom of Tharic, with its people known for their wisdom and endurance, had always been a bastion of strength. Yet, Aric, barely past his youth, found himself caught between the legacy of his ancestors and the demands of a world that grew darker by the day.

The prince roamed the royal gardens, his face etched with worry as he passed under the canopy of towering oaks and beneath the flowering vines that tangled like nature's own tapestry. The scent of blooming roses mixed with the earthy smell of damp soil, but the beauty of the garden did little to ease the heaviness in Aric's heart. His father, the king, lay bedridden with a mysterious ailment that no healer could explain or cure. The fate of Tharic now rested on Aric's young shoulders.

Aric's mother, Queen Elara, walked beside him, her own face a mask of strength and sorrow. She placed a hand on her son's shoulder, feeling the tension beneath his royal robes. "My son, the time has come for you to prove yourself. The people look to you for guidance and strength."

Aric nodded, his mind racing with the weight of his new responsibilities. He was young, inexperienced, and burdened with the knowledge that his father's illness left a void that could not be easily filled. The kingdom had always relied on the wisdom of the old king, a ruler who had weathered many storms and led Tharic with a steady hand. Now, with the king's health failing, the young prince had to step into a role for which he felt unprepared.

The prince's days were filled with meetings with advisors, each one offering their counsel with a mixture of respect and hidden agendas. The elders of Tharic, wise and seasoned, spoke of strategies and alliances, but Aric could see through their words. Their advice was often tinged with their own ambitions, and the young prince struggled to discern what was best for his people amidst the sea of conflicting interests.

One evening, as twilight draped its soft cloak over the kingdom, Aric found himself in the castle's library, surrounded by the ancient tomes and scrolls that held the history and lore of Tharic. He poured over the texts, searching for wisdom that might guide him through the turbulent times ahead. The flicker of candlelight cast dancing shadows on the walls, and the silence of the library was both comforting and daunting.

The old librarian, a man with a face as wrinkled as the scrolls he tended, approached with a gentle step. "Your Highness," he said, his voice soft and respectful, "you seek answers in the past. Perhaps it is not the past but the present that holds the key."

Aric looked up, his eyes weary. "What do you mean?"

The librarian's gaze was steady. "The strength of Tharic lies not only in its history but in its people. You are the future of this kingdom, and the burden you carry is not only of leadership but of understanding those you lead. Your true challenge is not just to rule but to connect with your people."

Aric took the librarian's words to heart. The next day, he ventured beyond the castle walls, mingling with the common folk in the bustling marketplace. He spoke with merchants, listened to farmers, and watched children play. The voices of the people were filled with concerns and hopes, their lives woven into the fabric of the kingdom. Aric felt a pang of guilt as he realized how detached he had been from the everyday struggles of his subjects.

During one such visit, he met an old woman who sold herbs and remedies. Her eyes, sharp and knowing, met his with a mixture of curiosity and respect. "Young prince," she said, "the burden you carry is great, but do not forget that true leadership is born from understanding and empathy. A king must not only lead but also listen."

Her words echoed in Aric's mind as he returned to the castle, where the weight of his role pressed down on him once more. The meetings with advisors and the strategic discussions were necessary, but Aric now saw them through a new lens. He needed to balance the demands of governance with the needs of his people.

The prince continued his visits to the kingdom, each time gaining more insight into the lives of his subjects. He began to make decisions not solely based on the advice of his council but also on the needs and desires of the people. The kingdom's well-being became a living, breathing entity in his mind, not just a set of figures and reports.

Despite his efforts, the path was not without its challenges. There were those who doubted his abilities, and the darkening sky cast a shadow over every decision. Yet, Aric's determination grew stronger. He realized that leadership was not just about bearing a burden but about rising to meet it with courage and compassion.

One night, as the moonlight bathed the castle in its silver glow, Aric stood on the balcony overlooking the kingdom. The lights of the village twinkled like stars scattered across the land, and the cool breeze carried the scent of the night air. The prince took a deep breath, feeling the weight of his role but also the strength that came from his connection to the people.

His mother, Queen Elara, joined him on the balcony. She placed a hand on his shoulder, a gesture of support and pride. "You have grown into your role, my son. The kingdom sees not just a ruler but a leader who cares for their well-being."

Aric turned to her, his eyes reflecting a newfound resolve. "I will continue to listen and learn. The burden I carry is great, but with the support of my people, I believe we can face whatever comes."

The darkening sky was still a threat, but Aric faced it with a renewed sense of purpose. The young prince had come to understand that true leadership was not just about bearing a crown but about connecting with those he led. As he looked out over the land, he felt a sense of hope and determination. The future of Tharic rested in his hands, and he would carry that burden with both strength and compassion, guided by the wisdom he had gained from both the past and the present.

Chapter 6

Shadows of Nocturne

Nocturne, a land where the very essence of darkness seemed to seep from the earth, the shadows moved with a life of their own. The realm was a place of perpetual twilight, where the sun barely pierced the thick, murky clouds that cloaked the land. Here, the people lived not in the light but in the embrace of the ever-present shadow.

Deep within the heart of Nocturne, in a fortress carved from the black stone of the mountains, the ruler of this somber land, Lord Malakar, prepared for a council of great import. His fortress, a labyrinth of darkened halls and echoing chambers, was alive with the murmurs of his advisors and the rustle of dark robes. The air was heavy with a sense of anticipation, a feeling that something significant was about to unfold.

Lord Malakar, draped in robes of deep crimson that seemed to drink in the light, sat upon a throne that was as much a symbol of power as it was a dark, foreboding presence. His eyes, like twin orbs of obsidian, scanned the room with a piercing gaze. The shadows danced around him, shifting and swirling as though they were extensions of his will. His presence commanded respect and fear, and even the most seasoned of his advisors shifted uneasily under his gaze.

The council began with a shuffling of feet and the clinking of goblets. Malakar's advisor, a gaunt figure with hollow eyes named Vesper, stepped forward. "My lord," he began, his voice a whisper that seemed to merge with the shadows, "the emissaries from the other kingdoms have arrived. They bring tidings of both hope and tension."

Malakar's lips curled into a smile that held no warmth. "Indeed. Let them come. The time has come for us to reveal our own hand in this game of shadows."

The emissaries entered, each one stepping into the darkness of the chamber with a mix of caution and determination. They came from distant lands, their expressions a blend of curiosity and wariness. Among them was Lady Seraphine, a sorceress from Aelarion whose presence seemed to light up the room despite the pervasive gloom. Her eyes, bright with an inner fire, scanned the room with a mixture of defiance and resolve.

Beside her was the emissary from Eryndor, a tall figure with an air of stoic determination. The emissary's eyes met Malakar's with a steady gaze, betraying nothing of the fears or doubts that might lie beneath the surface. From Tharic came a young noble, whose sharp gaze and poised demeanor spoke of a desire for alliances yet tempered with suspicion. The emissary from Valdor, a grizzled warrior with a scarred face, entered with the confidence of one accustomed to battle.

Malakar's voice cut through the murmur of introductions. "Welcome to Nocturne. We have much to discuss, for the shadows grow long, and the storm on the horizon draws near."

The emissaries took their seats, and the council commenced. The discussions were filled with tension as each representative laid out their kingdom's position and concerns. The shadows in the room seemed to pulse with the intensity of the debate, growing thicker with each passing moment.

Lady Seraphine was the first to speak, her voice carrying an edge of defiance. "The darkness that threatens us all is not just a mere shadow. It is a force that seeks to consume everything. Aelarion offers its magic, but we need more than just promises. We need action."

Malakar's eyes gleamed with a mix of amusement and challenge. "Magic can only do so much. The shadows of Nocturne are ancient and powerful. We have our own ways of dealing with darkness. What assurances can you give us that your lands will not falter under the strain?"

The emissary from Eryndor, his voice calm and measured, spoke next. "We understand the power of the shadows, but we also know the strength of unity. We must forge a plan that combines our strengths. No one kingdom can stand alone."

The young noble from Tharic nodded in agreement. "Tharic's people are resilient and resourceful. We will lend our support, but we must be sure that our efforts are met with equal commitment from all."

The grizzled warrior from Valdor grunted in agreement, his eyes reflecting the weight of battle-hardened experience. "Our strength lies in our resolve. We will fight alongside you, but we must trust that all parties are equally committed to the cause."

As the council continued, the discussions grew heated. The emissaries voiced their concerns, and Malakar listened with a mixture of curiosity and calculation. The shadows seemed to lean in, absorbing the words and weighing the promises made.

In the midst of the council, a disturbance arose. A figure emerged from the depths of the fortress, cloaked in dark robes that seemed to shimmer with a malevolent energy. The figure moved with a grace that was both unsettling and mesmerizing. The emissaries watched with a mix of fear and fascination as the figure approached Malakar.

The figure's voice was a soft murmur, barely audible over the din of the council. "My lord, the time has come for you to choose. The darkness grows stronger, and our allies must be tested. We must know who among them can be trusted and who may falter."

Malakar's eyes narrowed as he regarded the figure. "What do you suggest?"

The figure's gaze was inscrutable. "Let us test their resolve. Set a task that will reveal their true intentions. Only then will you know if they are worthy of your trust." Malakar considered this for a moment, then nodded. "Very well. We shall devise a test. The shadows shall reveal the truth."

As the council drew to a close, Malakar issued a challenge to the emissaries. Each kingdom would face a trial that would test their commitment and unity. The task would be difficult, but it was designed to expose any weaknesses or treachery among the allies.

The emissaries left the chamber, their faces marked with a mix of determination and unease. The shadows of Nocturne had cast their long reach over the proceedings, and the true nature of the alliances would soon be revealed. Malakar watched them go, his eyes reflecting the depth of the shadows that lay ahead.

In the darkened halls of Nocturne, the game of shadows continued. The emissaries would return to their lands, each carrying with them the weight of the trials to come. The true test of their alliances would unfold in the days ahead, and only time would tell if the combined strength of the kingdoms could withstand the encroaching darkness.

Chapter 7

The Council of Kings

The great hall of the ancient fortress, where the grand stone pillars seemed to whisper the secrets of ages past, the time had come for the Council of Kings to gather. The air was thick with anticipation, and the flickering torches cast long shadows that danced upon the walls. This was a moment that would echo through the annals of history, as rulers from distant lands convened to forge a path through the growing darkness.

The chamber was adorned with tapestries that depicted great battles and legendary heroes, their faded colors a testament to the tales they told. A massive oak table, scarred and weathered by time, stood at the center, its surface a battleground for the scrolls and maps that lay strewn across it. Around this table, the kings and their representatives took their places, each one bringing with them the weight of their realm and the hopes of their people.

King Eldric of Eryndor, his gaze sharp and resolute, surveyed the room. His kingdom was one of the sea and the storm, and the burden of leadership showed in the lines etched upon his face. Beside him, his trusted advisor stood ready, a silent sentinel who had seen the tides of many councils.

From Tharic came King Roderic, a figure of immense stature with a presence that seemed to fill the room. His kingdom, known for its rugged landscapes and resilient people, was represented by the king himself, a man whose experience and strength were beyond question.

The emissary from Aelarion, Lady Seraphine, arrived with an air of grace and determination. Her eyes, though they carried the weight of many battles fought in the realm of magic, sparkled with a fierce resolve.

The magic of Aelarion had always been a cornerstone of power, and her presence at the council was a testament to the seriousness of their plight.

Lord Malakar of Nocturne, shrouded in darkness and mystery, entered with an air of chilling authority. His realm was one of shadows and secrets, and his very presence seemed to draw the light from the room. His dark robes swept across the floor like tendrils of the night, and his eyes, deep and inscrutable, watched the proceedings with a quiet intensity.

The final arrival was King Darion of Valdor, a grizzled veteran with scars that spoke of countless battles. His kingdom's strength was renowned, and his reputation as a warrior was matched only by his wisdom in matters of state. He took his seat with a quiet dignity, his gaze fixed on the unfolding drama.

As the kings settled into their seats, the grand hall fell into a tense silence. The flickering torchlight played across the faces of the rulers, each one lost in thought as they prepared to address the council. The fate of their lands and the survival of their people rested upon the decisions made in this very room.

King Eldric rose first, his voice cutting through the silence with a tone of solemn authority. "Noble kings and leaders, we gather here not as separate realms but as one united front against the growing darkness. The time has come for us to speak openly and to lay aside our differences. Our world faces a threat that no single kingdom can withstand alone."

A murmur of agreement rippled through the room. King Roderic's voice, deep and resonant, followed. "Eryndor's call is wise. We have seen the signs and felt the encroaching shadows. Tharic stands ready to lend its strength, but we must be certain that our combined efforts will not falter."

Lady Seraphine, her voice carrying the weight of her realm's arcane knowledge, spoke next. "The magic of Aelarion has always been at your service. Yet, even our sorcery may not be enough if we are not united in purpose and action. We must forge a plan that brings together our strengths and resolves our differences."

Lord Malakar, his voice as soft and dark as the shadows that surrounded him, added his thoughts. "Nocturne has always thrived in the darkness, but even we cannot face this threat alone. The shadows hold many secrets, and we must trust each other if we are to uncover the true nature of the peril we face."

King Darion, his gaze steady and unwavering, spoke last. "Valdor's warriors are prepared for battle, but we cannot fight a shadow with mere strength. Our unity must be our greatest weapon. We must ensure that our alliances are forged in trust and that our strategies are sound."

The room fell silent again as the weight of the kings' words settled over them. The council had begun with a sense of urgency, but now the need for unity and clear strategy became even more apparent. The darkness that loomed was not just a threat to one kingdom but to all.

As the council continued, the discussions turned to the specifics of their alliance. Maps were spread out, showing the borders of each kingdom and the paths that lay between them. The kings and their advisors debated strategies, each contributing their knowledge and resources to the plan. The flickering torchlight revealed the intensity of their focus, the tension of their negotiations.

King Eldric suggested a coordinated defense, where each kingdom would protect its own borders while supporting the others. King Roderic proposed the creation of a central command, where representatives from each realm could oversee the joint efforts and ensure that no kingdom was left to fend for itself.

Lady Seraphine offered her realm's magic as a means to both strengthen defenses and uncover hidden threats. Lord Malakar's insight into the shadows was invaluable, providing crucial information about the nature of the darkness they faced. King Darion's experience in warfare helped to shape a strategy that balanced strength with strategy.

As the night wore on, the discussions grew more focused, and the plans began to take shape. The kings' voices, once filled with doubt and tension, now carried a note of resolve and determination. The darkness that had loomed over their lands was met with a united front, and the council of kings forged a path forward.

In the grand hall of the ancient fortress, the echoes of the Council of Kings would be remembered as a turning point in their struggle against the encroaching shadow. The rulers had come together, setting aside their differences for the greater good. As they left the chamber, their faces were marked with a mixture of hope and resolve, knowing that their united efforts would be tested in the days to come.

The grand hall, now quiet and empty, stood as a silent witness to the decisions made within its walls. The shadows that had once seemed so foreboding now held a glimmer of hope. The Council of Kings had set the stage for a battle against the darkness, and their combined strength would determine the fate of their lands and the world beyond.

Chapter 8

Betrayal in the Ranks

The Council of Kings had set forth their grand plan, a union of strength and strategy to face the encroaching darkness. Yet, amid the echoes of unity and promises, a dark twist awaited. As the cold moon cast its silver light over the land, whispers of discord and betrayal began to weave their way through the ranks. The grand halls of the fortresses, once filled with the sounds of collaboration and resolve, now bore witness to the murmurings of discontent and deceit.

It was within the heart of Tharic, among the ancient stone walls and towering battlements, that the first signs of betrayal began to surface. The kingdom's trusted general, a man of steel and honor named Corwin, had always been seen as a pillar of loyalty. Yet, beneath his steadfast exterior lay a heart touched by greed and discontent. He had long coveted more power, and the growing darkness offered him a dangerous opportunity. Corwin's scheming started subtly. Secret meetings with emissaries from rival realms, hidden letters exchanged under the cover of night, and whispers of discontent spread like wildfire through the ranks of Tharic's army. His betrayal was not born of hatred but of ambition and disillusionment. He felt that the grand alliance, though noble in its purpose, had left his kingdom vulnerable, and he saw an opportunity to carve out his own path to power.

In the shadows of Nocturne, Lord Malakar, ever the master of intrigue, sensed a shift in the currents of power. His spies, masters of concealment and deception, brought him tidings of Corwin's treachery. The dark lord, with eyes that saw through the veils of deceit, knew that the time had come to act. Malakar summoned his closest advisors, their faces hidden beneath dark hoods, and laid out the truth of Corwin's betrayal. "The darkness grows, and with it, the treachery within our ranks. Corwin seeks to undermine our efforts and seize control for himself. We must act swiftly to neutralize this threat."

The advisors nodded, their expressions grim as they prepared to deal with the traitor. Malakar's plan was ruthless and precise. He would expose Corwin's treachery in such a way that it would not only remove the threat but also send a clear message to any who might consider following in his footsteps.

The day came when Corwin's betrayal was to be revealed. The grand hall of Tharic was filled with the leaders of the kingdom, their faces a mix of anticipation and anxiety. Corwin, confident in his treachery, believed that his plans were flawless and that he had ensured his victory.

As the assembly gathered, a hush fell over the crowd. King Roderic, his face a mask of grim determination, addressed his subjects. "We have gathered here today to discuss the progress of our grand alliance and to strengthen our resolve. But there are matters of grave concern that must be addressed."

The doors to the grand hall swung open, and a procession of soldiers marched in, their steps echoing through the chamber. At their head was Malakar's emissary, holding a bundle of documents that revealed the depth of Corwin's betrayal. The crowd gasped as the documents were spread before them, detailing secret meetings, hidden alliances, and Corwin's plans to seize control of Tharic and undermine the grand alliance.

Corwin's face turned ashen as the evidence was laid bare. The room erupted into chaos as his former allies turned against him, their voices raised in anger and disbelief. The general, once a respected leader, now stood exposed and vulnerable, his ambitions unraveling before his eyes.

King Roderic's voice cut through the clamor. "Corwin, you stand accused of betrayal and treachery. Your actions have endangered the very people you swore to protect. What say you to these charges?"

Corwin, his pride and confidence shattered, tried to defend himself, but his words fell flat against the weight of the evidence. His pleas for mercy were met with cold stares and harsh judgment. The betrayal was not just a personal failure but a threat to the very fabric of the alliance they had worked so hard to build. The punishment for Corwin was swift and severe. He was stripped of his rank and cast out from Tharic, his name forever tainted by his treachery. The grand hall, once a place of unity and resolve, was now a reminder of the darkness that could fester within even the most trusted of allies.

As Corwin was led away, the leaders of the alliance gathered to regroup and reassess their plans. The betrayal had shaken their confidence, but it had also reinforced their resolve. They knew that the darkness they faced was not just a force of nature but a reflection of the corruption that could seep into even the most noble of causes.

In the wake of the betrayal, the alliance's efforts were redoubled. The leaders, though wary, worked together to strengthen their defenses and fortify their bonds. The darkening sky was still a threat, but the unity forged in the face of betrayal would become their greatest strength.

The tale of Corwin's betrayal spread across the land, serving as a stark reminder of the dangers that lay in wait for those who sought to undermine the greater good. The kingdoms, though scarred by the treachery, found renewed strength in their shared purpose. The shadows of betrayal had tested their resolve, but in their wake, they had forged an even stronger alliance.

As the darkness continued to encroach upon the world, the leaders of the grand alliance stood firm, their unity and determination a beacon of hope in the face of the gathering storm. The tale of betrayal and redemption would be told for generations, a testament to the resilience of those who, despite the shadows that threatened to tear them apart, stood together to face the darkness.

Chapter 9

The Rising Tide

Across the vast lands where kingdoms stretched their fingers past many realms, a rising tide was felt, not in the waves but in the hearts of those who stood at the brink of a storm. The once-clear skies grew heavy with dark clouds, and the whispers of the approaching tempest reached even the furthest corners of the world.

The day began like any other in the kingdom of Eryndor, where the sea, though often tumultuous, had always been a friend. But the morning brought with it an ominous stillness, as if the world was holding its breath. King Eldric stood upon the cliffs, his eyes scanning the horizon where the dark waters met the brooding sky. He sensed the change in the wind, a sign of the rising tide that would soon bring more than just waves.

In the fortress of Tharic, King Roderic paced the halls, his mind churning with the weight of the news that had come from the coast. The sea, once a boundary and protector, now seemed like a restless beast, ready to break its chains. Roderic, known for his unshakable resolve, felt the pressure of the storm gathering strength. His soldiers prepared, their faces marked by a mixture of determination and concern.

Far to the south in Aelarion, Lady Seraphine studied the magical omens that spoke of the approaching tide. Her realm, known for its arcane prowess, had sensed a shift in the balance of power. The ancient texts and mystical symbols foretold of a rising tide, not just of water, but of darkness that would challenge the very essence of their strength. Her heart, though resolute, beat with a foreboding rhythm as she prepared her people for what was to come.

In the shadowy halls of Nocturne, Lord Malakar's spies brought word of the turmoil spreading through the lands. The darkness that had always been a part of Nocturne now seemed to be stirring with a newfound intensity. Malakar, ever the master of shadows, understood that the rising tide was not merely a physical threat but a harbinger of the coming darkness. His mind worked swiftly, crafting plans within the depths of his fortress.

King Darion of Valdor, a seasoned warrior with scars that told tales of battle, felt the tremors of the rising tide through his very bones. The earth itself seemed to shiver with the anticipation of the storm. Valdor's preparations were underway, as the kingdom's mighty warriors readied themselves for the clash that would soon come. Darion knew that the tide would test the strength and unity of their alliance like never before.

As the rising tide made its presence known, the leaders of the alliance gathered once more. Their meeting was held in a grand hall that had witnessed many discussions of strategy and unity. But this time, the atmosphere was charged with urgency and anxiety. The threat was no longer a distant concern but an immediate danger that loomed over them.

The grand hall was filled with maps and charts, each one detailing the progress of the storm and its impact on their realms. The leaders examined the rising waters, the growing darkness, and the shifting patterns that foretold of the challenges ahead. Their faces were etched with concern as they realized the scale of the threat that loomed over their lands.

King Eldric spoke first, his voice steady but tinged with worry. "The rising tide is more than just a natural event. It is a sign of the upheaval that is coming. We must prepare ourselves for the worst and strengthen our defenses."

King Roderic, his face grim, nodded in agreement. "Our lands are vulnerable, and the sea's rage could bring destruction to our shores. We must fortify our defenses and ensure that our people are ready for the storm."

Lady Seraphine, her eyes glowing with determination, added, "Magic alone may not hold back the tide, but it can help us understand and prepare for the darkness that accompanies it. We must use every tool at our disposal."

Lord Malakar's voice, as dark and deep as the shadows he commanded, spoke next. "The rising tide is a sign that the darkness is growing stronger. We must be vigilant and ready to confront whatever emerges from the shadows."

King Darion, his voice filled with the weight of experience, concluded, "Our strength lies in our unity. We must stand together and face this storm with resolve and courage."

As the leaders discussed their strategy, the rising tide became a symbol of the challenges they would face together. The water's advance mirrored the growing darkness that threatened to consume their lands. The leaders knew that their combined strength and determination would be tested like never before.

The days that followed were filled with frantic preparations. The shores of Eryndor were fortified with barriers and watchtowers. Tharic's warriors trained harder, readying themselves for any assault from the sea. Aelarion's magic was harnessed to protect against the encroaching darkness, while Nocturne's shadows were used to gather intelligence and prepare for the unknown.

Valdor's forces assembled, their might and discipline ready to face the storm. The rising tide was not just a force of nature but a challenge that would test their unity and resolve. The leaders worked tirelessly, knowing that the strength of their alliance would be their greatest weapon against the gathering storm.

As the tide rose and the storm approached, the leaders gathered once more to assess their preparations. The skies were now a roiling mass of dark clouds, and the waters churned with a ferocity that spoke of the tempest to come. The alliance stood on the brink, their resolve as steadfast as the walls they had built.

The rising tide was more than just a physical threat; it was a challenge that would test the very foundation of their unity. The storm that loomed on the horizon was a reminder of the darkness that threatened to engulf their lands. But in the face of this rising tide, the leaders of the alliance stood firm, their strength and determination shining through the gathering storm.

As the waters rose and the storm raged, the fate of the kingdoms would be decided by their ability to stand together and face the challenges that lay ahead. The rising tide was a test of their unity, and their response would determine the future of their realms and the world beyond.

Chapter 10

Bonds of War

The world was thrown into turmoil as the storm approached, dark clouds billowing like a furious beast ready to devour the land. The kingdoms, once separate and distinct, were now bound together by the urgency of war. The tides of fate had brought them to this moment, where their combined strength would be tested against the rising storm of conflict.

In the fortress of Eryndor, King Eldric stood amidst his warriors, his eyes fixed on the horizon where the storm clouds gathered. The sea roared in defiance, as if it, too, was preparing for the coming battle. Eldric's armor gleamed under the fiery sunset, and his voice rang out with the power of a leader who understood the weight of the burden upon his shoulders. His people gathered, their faces set in grim determination, knowing that the time for preparation was over. The bonds of war had forged a new unity among them.

To the north, in the rugged land of Tharic, King Roderic's army readied itself with the discipline of seasoned warriors. The clang of weapons and the murmur of battle plans filled the air. Roderic, a figure of resolute strength, moved among his soldiers, his presence a beacon of courage. The warriors of Tharic, once mere subjects of a kingdom, had become comrades in arms, their loyalty to each other now unbreakable. They were bound by the common cause of defending their land and their newfound allies.

In the realm of Aelarion, Sorceress Queen of Aelarion with her trusted aid Lady Seraphine's magical preparations reached their peak. The ancient texts and arcane rituals wove together the threads of magic that would shield their kingdom from the darkness. Aelarion's magic was no longer a mere tool but a symbol of their shared struggle. The sorcerers and enchantresses worked side by side with the warriors, their bond of magic and steel strengthening their resolve. They knew that their mystical prowess would be the key to turning the tide of war.

Nocturne's shadowy corridors were alive with activity as Lord Malakar's spies and operatives prepared for the coming conflict. The darkness that once served as a shroud now became a cloak of protection for those who moved through it. Malakar's realm, always shrouded in secrecy, had transformed into a hub of strategic planning. His spies reported on the movements of enemies and allies alike, their information forming the backbone of the alliance's strategy. The bonds of war had united them in their purpose, making their efforts more synchronized and effective.

In Valdor, King Darion's seasoned warriors gathered, their ranks filled with fighters who had seen many battles. The warhorns blared, signaling the readiness of an army forged through countless trials. Darion's leadership had turned his kingdom into a symbol of resilience and strength. His warriors, bound by their loyalty to their king and their commitment to the alliance, stood ready to face the storm. The bonds of war had turned them from mere soldiers into a formidable force, prepared to stand against any foe.

As the storm drew nearer, the alliance's leaders convened to finalize their plans. The grand hall of the meeting place was filled with maps and charts, each one detailing the strategies they had devised. The leaders' faces were set in grim determination as they reviewed their plans, knowing that every decision would impact the outcome of the coming battle. The bonds of war were evident in the way the leaders communicated and collaborated. There were no longer mere alliances but a deep, unshakeable unity forged in the crucible of shared danger. The leaders, once bound by diplomacy and duty, now stood as comrades in arms, their strategies and preparations a testament to their unity.

King Eldric spoke with a voice that carried the weight of their combined effort. "We have prepared for this day, and now we must face the storm together. Our strength lies in our unity, and our bonds of war will see us through."

King Roderic, his face lined with the marks of a lifetime of battle, nodded in agreement. "Our warriors are ready, and our defenses are strong. We must stand as one and fight with the resolve that has brought us together."

Lady Seraphine's voice, filled with the power of magic and determination, added, "The darkness may be strong, but our magic will shield us. We must use every advantage we have and stand firm against the rising tide."

Lord Malakar, his eyes glinting with the knowledge of shadows and secrets, spoke next. "The darkness will test us, but our preparations and unity will be our greatest strength. We are bound by our purpose, and that purpose will guide us through the storm."

King Darion, his voice resonant with the authority of a seasoned leader, concluded, "The bonds we have forged in this time of war will be our greatest asset. We will face the storm together, and our combined strength will see us through."

With the leaders' words of resolve, the alliance prepared to face the rising tide. The storm, both literal and metaphorical, would test their unity and their resolve. The bonds of war had turned disparate kingdoms into a single, formidable force, ready to confront the darkness that threatened their lands.

As the armies took their positions and the magical barriers were put into place, the storm loomed ever closer. The alliance stood ready, their strength and unity a beacon of hope against the gathering darkness. The bonds of war had forged a new era of cooperation and courage, and the coming battle would be a testament to their shared resolve. The leaders and their people, bound by a common cause, stood firm against the storm, their unity and determination shining through the darkness.

Chapter 11

The Prophecy Unfolds

The land lay still, gripped by the heavy silence that precedes great events. The storm had raged, and the armies had clashed, but the skies held their secrets close, as if waiting for the right moment to reveal the truth. The time had come for the prophecy, long whispered in hushed tones and written in ancient tomes, to unfold before the eyes of those who stood at the crossroads of fate.

In the heart of Eryndor, the grand hall was abuzz with the restless murmurs of those who had witnessed the storm's fury and the battle's aftermath. King Eldric, his face etched with the lines of worry and determination, stood before a grand tapestry that depicted a prophecy known to few. The tapestry's threads seemed to shimmer with a life of their own, and the figures woven into it appeared to shift and move with the telling of the tale.

The prophecy had long been a source of both hope and fear. It spoke of a time when darkness would rise, threatening to consume the world, and of a hero who would emerge to wield the power to turn the tide. Eldric, with his gaze fixed on the tapestry, could feel the weight of destiny pressing upon him. The time had come to see if the threads of the prophecy would align with the events unfolding before them.

To the east, in the realm of Aelarion, Lady Seraphine and her council of sorcerers gathered around an ancient scroll. The scroll, covered in mystical runes and symbols, had been the subject of much study and speculation. Its secrets were believed to hold the key to understanding the prophecy's true meaning. As Seraphine's fingers traced the runes, the air crackled with magic, and the scroll seemed to pulse with a hidden energy.

The prophecy spoke of an artifact, lost to the ages, that would be found and wielded by the chosen one. This artifact, a crystal imbued with ancient power, was said to be hidden in a place known only to the prophecy's bearer. The sorcerers, their faces marked with the strain of their task, knew that the time to find this artifact was at hand. The rising darkness had made it clear that their role in the prophecy was about to come to fruition.

In the shadowy realm of Nocturne, Lord Malakar watched with keen interest. His spies had brought word of the prophecy's latest developments, and the dark lord knew that the unfolding events would have far-reaching consequences. Malakar's fortress, always cloaked in shadows, now seemed even darker as he contemplated the prophecy's implications. The dark lord's plans, always shrouded in secrecy, were now focused on ensuring that the prophecy did not lead to his downfall.

Malakar understood that the prophecy was not merely a prediction but a challenge that must be met with cunning and strategy. His spies and operatives were dispatched to gather more information and to ensure that the dark forces he commanded would be prepared for whatever came next. The prophecy's unfolding was a signal that the time for decisive action had arrived.

Far to the north, in the rugged land of Valdor, King Darion and his warriors stood ready. The prophecy had spoken of a time when the might of warriors would be needed to defend against the darkness. Darion, with his seasoned troops, knew that their strength and discipline would be tested like never before. The rising threat had united them with the other kingdoms, and their readiness was a testament to the bonds forged in the fires of war.

Darion's warriors, their faces set in grim determination, prepared for the challenges ahead. The prophecy had become more than a distant tale; it was a call to arms that demanded their full commitment. The strength of Valdor's forces was now intertwined with the fates of the other realms, and their role in the prophecy was one of crucial importance.

ALLIED THRONES: THE LAST PACT

As the pieces of the prophecy came together, the leaders gathered once more to discuss their next steps. The grand hall of Eryndor, once a place of strategic meetings, had become a sanctuary for those who sought to understand the unfolding prophecy. The leaders, their faces a mix of resolve and apprehension, met to share their insights and to plan their course of action.

Eldric, with the tapestry as a backdrop, spoke of the prophecy's meaning and the role each kingdom was to play. "The tapestry reveals that the time has come for the prophecy to unfold. We must understand the true nature of the artifact and the hero who will wield its power."

Lady Seraphine, her eyes bright with determination, added, "The scroll has revealed that the artifact is hidden and that we must find it before the darkness grows stronger. Our magic will guide us in this quest."

Lord Malakar's voice, always measured and precise, echoed through the hall. "The darkness will not wait for us to act. We must be prepared for any move and ensure that our plans are in place to counter the prophecy's outcome."

King Darion, his voice firm and commanding, concluded, "Our warriors are ready, and our resolve is strong. We will stand together and face the challenges that come with the prophecy."

The leaders' words were a promise of unity and determination. The prophecy's unfolding was not merely a prediction but a call to action. The artifact, the hero, and the darkness were all part of a grand narrative that would shape the fate of the realms. The bonds forged in war and the alliances formed in times of peril were now tested against the backdrop of the prophecy's demands.

As the days passed, the search for the artifact became a quest that united the realms in a common cause. The leaders, their forces, and their magical resources were focused on finding the artifact and ensuring that the prophecy's outcome would be one of victory rather than defeat. The storm that had once threatened to consume the world now seemed to be the backdrop to a larger tale, one that would be remembered for generations to come.

The prophecy had unfolded, and with it came the realization that their actions and decisions would shape the future. The leaders and their people stood at the threshold of destiny, their fates intertwined with the ancient predictions that had guided their steps. The unfolding of the prophecy was a reminder of the power of unity, courage, and determination in the face of darkness.

The artifact, the hero, and the prophecy's final revelations were still to be discovered, but the bonds formed through their trials had prepared them for whatever lay ahead. The prophecy had become a beacon, guiding their actions and decisions as they faced the challenges of the coming days. In the grand tapestry of fate, their roles were set, and the story of their struggle and triumph would be woven into the annals of history.

Chapter 12

Allies and Adversaries

The winds carried whispers of war across the land, rustling the leaves of ancient trees and stirring the waters of the deep seas. The kingdoms, once isolated and content within their borders, were now bound together by a threat that loomed over them all. The halls of Aelarion, Valdor, Eryndor, Tharic, and Nocturne buzzed with the tension of battle preparations, as each kingdom steeled itself for the coming storm. Trust was a fragile thing, tested by the weight of old grudges and the uncertainty of new alliances.

King Eldric of Eryndor, known for his sharp mind and the strength of his navy, found himself surrounded by the leaders of the allied kingdoms in the grand hall of his coastal fortress. The sea outside churned with the fury of an approaching tempest, mirroring the unease that gripped the rulers within.

Lady Seraphine of Aelarion, the land where magic thrived and mystical creatures roamed freely, stood tall, her silver hair glowing under the dim light of the hall. Her eyes, bright and full of wisdom, scanned the room, taking in each face with a calm yet calculating gaze. The elves of Aelarion had long kept to themselves, their magic a closely guarded secret, but now, with the world on the brink of chaos, they had stepped forward, their power a crucial force in the alliance.

Beside her, King Darion of Valdor, a land of fierce warriors, clenched his fists in silent anticipation. His people were known for their indomitable spirit, forged in the crucible of countless battles. The scars on his hands were a testament to his own experience on the battlefield, and his heart beat with the desire to lead his warriors into the fray once more. But this time, the enemy was more than just a rival kingdom, it was a darkness that threatened to consume them all.

King Roderic of Tharic was a stark contrast to the others. His realm was rich in resources, its wealth built on the backs of skilled artisans and traders. His mind was as sharp as the finest blade, and his economy was the envy of many. Yet, despite his material wealth, he understood that this battle could not be won with gold alone. The craftsmen of Tharic had begun forging weapons and armor, their skills put to the test as they prepared for a war unlike any other.

And then there was Nocturne, the kingdom shrouded in mystery and shadow. Its ruler, Lord Malakar, was a figure of whispers and rumors. No one truly knew the extent of his power or the secrets he harbored, but it was said that Nocturne held the key to tipping the balance of power in this war. Lord Malakar's presence in the hall was a quiet one, his eyes hidden beneath the shadow of his hood, but his influence was palpable. The other rulers could not afford to trust him completely, but they could not afford to ignore him either. The tension in the hall was thick as Eldric spoke, his voice echoing off the stone walls. "We stand on the brink of a war that will decide the fate of all our kingdoms. The darkness we face is not one that can be fought with swords and shields alone. We must stand together, or we will fall divided."

Lady Seraphine nodded, her voice as smooth as silk. "Aelarion's magic is at your disposal, Eldric. Our sorcerers have been preparing spells to shield our armies and strike at the heart of our enemies. But we must be careful. Magic is a powerful tool, but it is also unpredictable."

King Darion slammed his fist on the table, his patience wearing thin. "Magic is well and good, but my warriors crave the heat of battle! Valdor will not sit idly by while others fight our war. We will march at the front, as we always have."

King Roderic raised a hand, his tone measured. "And what of the supplies, the weapons, the armor? My kingdom has the resources, but we cannot afford to waste them. We must plan our strategy carefully, or we will exhaust our strength before the final blow is struck."

All eyes turned to Lord Malakar, who had remained silent until now. He finally spoke, his voice a low murmur that sent shivers down the spines of those present. "Nocturne will provide what is needed...when the time is right. The shadows of my kingdom are not to be underestimated. But know this: our allegiance is not given lightly, and it can be withdrawn just as easily." The room fell into an uneasy silence. The alliance was a fragile one, held together by the shared threat of annihilation, but weakened by the mistrust that simmered beneath the surface. Each ruler knew that their kingdom's survival depended on the others, yet none could fully place their faith in their fellow allies.

Eldric stood, his gaze sweeping across the gathered rulers. "We have no choice but to trust each other, as much as it may go against our instincts. This war will test us in ways we cannot yet imagine. But if we falter now, all is lost. We must move forward as one, or we will surely fall as many."

The rulers nodded in agreement, though the doubt remained in their eyes. The path ahead was uncertain, and the alliances they had forged were as fragile as the peace that had once reigned across their lands. But they had made their choice, and there was no turning back.

Outside the fortress, the storm finally broke, the skies opening up in a torrent of rain and lightning. It was as if the very heavens were weeping for the blood that would soon be spilled, the lives that would be lost in the struggle for survival. But within the walls of Eryndor, the rulers of the five kingdoms stood resolute, their minds set on the battles to come.

The war was far from over, and the alliances that had been forged in the fires of necessity would be tested to their limits. But as long as they stood together, as long as they fought with all their strength, there was still hope. The darkness might be vast and terrifying, but the light of their unity, however flickering, could yet guide them through.

And so, the allied kingdoms of Aelarion, Valdor, Eryndor, Tharic, and Nocturne prepared to face the oncoming storm.

Chapter 13

The Battle for Unity

In the cold light of dawn, as the first rays of sunlight pierced the veil of night, the battlefield stretched out like a scar upon the land. The allied forces, a tapestry of banners and armor, readied themselves for the clash that would determine their fate. The ground, churned and bloodied, bore witness to the countless struggles that had led to this moment.

The Warrior King of Valdor, his armor glinting in the pale light, stood at the head of his troops. King Darion's face was set in a grim line, his eyes scanning the horizon where the enemy was beginning to take shape. His warriors, fierce and battle-hardened, awaited his command, their spirits high despite the uncertainty that hung in the air. Darion's mind was troubled; the memories of old grudges and past betrayals weighed heavily upon him. Trust was a hard-earned prize, and though he valued honor above all, the idea of depending on former foes gnawed at him.

To his left, the Sorceress Queen of Aelarion, her presence commanding and regal, raised her staff to the heavens. Lady Seraphine, her closest confidant, stood beside her, her expression a blend of determination and unease. The Sorceress Queen's eyes, dark and deep as the abyss, were filled with a sadness born from a prophecy that haunted her dreams. Her magic, powerful and ancient, crackled in the air, a shimmering shield against the darkness that threatened their unity.

Across from them, King Eldric paced with a restless energy. King Eldric's thoughts were a storm of strategy and emotions. He was a master negotiator, but the pull of forbidden love wove a complicated thread through his duty. His navy, poised and ready, would soon take to the waters if needed. But for now, his gaze was fixed on the battlefield, his mind torn between the demands of his kingdom and the heart's clandestine desires.

Nearby, the Young Heir of Tharic, thrust into leadership by the untimely death of his predecessor, stood with a resolve that belied his inexperience. King Roderic, though young and unseasoned, was determined to prove himself. His artisans had provided the finest weapons and armor, and now it was time for him to lead his people in battle. The weight of leadership was heavy upon his shoulders, but his courage shone through the uncertainty.

In the shadows, the enigmatic figure of the Shadow Prince of Nocturne observed the scene with an inscrutable gaze. Lord Malakar's dark robes billowed around him as his army, cloaked in secrecy and shadow, prepared for their own part in the coming conflict. No one fully understood Malakar's true intentions or his connection to the dark force threatening the world. His presence was a silent, brooding enigma that added an element of unpredictability to the already volatile situation.

As the sun rose higher, the enemy's forces emerged from the mist, a sprawling mass of dark shapes and menacing forms. They were a chaotic tide, moving with a disturbing fluidity that suggested an intelligence behind their menace. The air was thick with the promise of violence, and the allied forces braced themselves for the onslaught.

The battle began with a roar that shook the heavens. Valdor's warriors surged forward, their swords gleaming as they met the enemy's advance. King Darion's voice cut through the din, rallying his men with a battle cry that echoed across the plain. The clash of steel was a thunderous symphony, the ground quaking beneath the fury of combat.

Aelarion's magic illuminated the battlefield with a fierce, radiant glow. The Sorceress Queen's spells wove a protective barrier around her allies, while Lady Seraphine channeled her own formidable power into devastating attacks. The magic was a beacon against the encroaching darkness, its brilliance momentarily driving back the enemy's forces.

The Diplomat Prince's navy, having waited in the wings, launched their attack from the waters. The cannons roared, their shots tearing through the enemy lines and creating chaos among their ranks. King Eldric stood at the helm, his eyes scanning the shifting tides of battle, ready to adapt his strategy as the fight evolved.

Tharic's soldiers fought with precision and skill, their weapons and armor a testament to their craftsmen's expertise. The Young Heir, though inexperienced, demonstrated a keen tactical mind, guiding his troops with a determination that inspired those around him. The resources and preparation of Tharic proved their worth on the battlefield.

And then there was Nocturne. Lord Malakar's forces moved with an eerie, calculated grace, their dark magic a chilling counterpoint to the brilliance of Aelarion's spells. Shadows danced around them, and their presence seemed to shift the very air with an unsettling force. Malakar's intentions remained a mystery, but his army's dark power was unmistakable.

The battle raged on, a fierce and unrelenting struggle. Each kingdom faced its own challenges, its own enemies, but their combined strength was formidable. The unity they had fought so hard to achieve was tested in every clash of steel and surge of magic.

Victory was not granted easily. The enemy was relentless, and the struggle to maintain unity among the allied forces was as fierce as the battle itself. Each ruler played a crucial role, their armies working together to push back the tide of darkness that threatened to consume them. As the sun began to set, the battlefield fell silent. The enemy, their forces broken and scattered, retreated into the shadows from whence they came. The allied armies stood victorious, their banners still waving in the dying light, a testament to their unity and strength.

The cost of the battle was high. Scars of combat marked every warrior, every ruler. Yet, they had achieved what seemed impossible—a united front against a darkness that had sought to destroy them. The battle for unity was won, but the war was far from over. The shadows that lurked on the edges of their world were not easily vanquished.

With the enemy driven back and the promise of peace hanging in the balance, the rulers of Aelarion, Valdor, Eryndor, Tharic, and Nocturne took a moment to reflect on their hard-won victory. Their unity had been tested, and they had emerged stronger for it. The battle for unity was a chapter in their story, but the story itself was far from finished.

Each step forward was a step towards a future where their combined strength could stand against the darkness and forge a lasting peace. The allied forces had proven their resilience and their courage, but the path ahead was fraught with challenges. The battle for unity had set the stage for the next chapter in their saga, a chapter that would define their legacy in the annals of history.

Chapter 14

The Price of Peace

In the wake of the fierce battle that marked the triumph of unity, the land lay quiet, bruised yet hopeful. The allied kingdoms, weary but victorious, turned their eyes to the horizon, where the promise of peace beckoned like a distant, shimmering dream. Yet, the price of this hard-won peace was about to become clear, and the cost would be measured in more than just the toll of battle.

King Darion of Valdor, the Warrior King, stood at the edge of his castle, overlooking the vast fields where the blood of his people had mingled with the soil. His heart, though fierce and true, carried a heavy burden. Honor demanded that he led his people with strength and resolve, but now, the weight of peace rested on his shoulders. Trust was a fragile thing, and while victory had united the allies in battle, old wounds and grievances simmered beneath the surface. Darion knew that forging lasting peace meant more than just defeating an enemy—it meant mending the rifts that had long divided them.

In the halls of Aelarion, the Sorceress Queen faced her own trial. The shadows of the prophecy lingered, whispering secrets of loss and sorrow. The battle had been a testament to her strength, but the cost had left deep scars. Magic had protected them, but the price of wielding such power was steep. Lady Seraphine, her trusted ally, shared the burden of these dark secrets, their bond forged in the fires of conflict. The kingdom's prosperity now hinged on whether the queen could find solace and balance, or if the prophecy would continue to cast its long shadow over her rule.

King Eldric, grappled with a different kind of challenge. His navy had proven its might, but his heart was a battlefield of its own. The forbidden love that had once been a private torment now threatened to unravel the delicate fabric of diplomacy. Eldric's role as a master negotiator was critical, but the strain of balancing personal desires with the needs of his kingdom created a storm that raged within him. The peace they sought to build required more than tactical acumen; it needed a heart that could navigate the treacherous waters of love and loyalty.

King Roderic of Tharic, though young and inexperienced, had demonstrated his courage in battle. Now, the true test of his leadership lay in the aftermath. The resources of Tharic had played a crucial role in the victory, but the cost of war had left the kingdom depleted. His artisans, who had crafted the finest weapons and armor, now faced the task of rebuilding a realm that had been ravaged by conflict. Roderic's determination would be tested as he sought to restore his kingdom's strength while grappling with the consequences of their victory.

In the shadows, Lord Malakar of Nocturne watched the aftermath with a calculating gaze. His dark forces had fought alongside the allies, yet his true motives remained shrouded in mystery. The price of peace for Nocturne was not merely measured in the battles fought but in the enigmatic plans that Malakar had yet to unveil. The dark forces that had once threatened the world were now allies, but their allegiance came with a price. Malakar's true intentions were a puzzle that no one could yet solve, and the peace they sought might come with hidden costs.

As the kingdoms began the arduous task of rebuilding and forging new alliances, the toll of their shared struggle became apparent. The land bore scars of battle, and the people, though resilient, carried the marks of the conflict in their hearts. The price of peace was not just the cost of war but the sacrifices made and the trust that had to be earned anew.

The rulers convened in a grand assembly, their faces reflecting the weight of their responsibilities. The halls of diplomacy, once echoing with the clamor of war, now resonated with a quiet intensity. Each ruler had their own vision for the future, and their united front was a fragile alliance built on both hope and necessity. The discussions were fraught with tension as they navigated the delicate balance of power and trust.

King Darion's voice, solemn and commanding, called for unity among the allies. He spoke of the sacrifices made and the need to honor those who had fallen. His words, though heartfelt, were met with a mix of hope and skepticism. The scars of war were fresh, and the path to lasting peace was uncertain.

The Sorceress Queen, her presence as commanding as ever, spoke of the need for healing and reconciliation. Her magic had been a beacon in the darkness, but the cost had been great. She urged her fellow rulers to look beyond the immediate gains and focus on building a future where their peoples could thrive together.

King Eldric, with a heavy heart, addressed the assembly with the wisdom born of his own trials. His words carried the weight of both his kingdom's strategic needs and his personal struggles. He spoke of the importance of trust and the need to navigate the complex web of alliances with care and integrity.

King Roderic, young yet determined, added his voice to the chorus of leaders. He spoke of the future of Tharic, of the need to rebuild and restore what had been lost. His vision was one of hope and renewal, a call to his allies to support each other in the difficult times ahead.

And in the shadows, Lord Malakar watched with a gaze that revealed nothing. His presence was a reminder of the dark forces that still lingered, their true nature hidden behind a veil of alliance. The price of peace was not yet fully revealed, and the path ahead was fraught with uncertainties.

The assembly concluded with a sense of cautious optimism. The rulers had spoken, and the first steps toward peace were taken. Yet, the price of this peace was not merely in the aftermath of battle but in the ongoing struggle to build a future where unity and trust could flourish.

As the sun set on this chapter of their story, the kingdoms faced the challenge of turning their hard-won victory into a lasting peace. The cost had been high, and the path ahead was uncertain, but the determination of the rulers and the strength of their alliances were a beacon of hope in a world that had been forever changed.

Chapter 15

A New Dawn

The day began with a whispering breeze that rustled through the trees, carrying the promise of new beginnings. The once war-torn lands now bathed in the soft light of dawn, a gentle reminder that after the storm, there comes calm. The allied kingdoms, their spirits scarred but unbroken, woke to a world that was forever changed.

King Darion of Valdor stood on the balcony of his castle, his eyes tracing the horizon where the first rays of sunlight kissed the earth. The night's battles were a memory now, replaced by the golden hues of dawn. He had seen his kingdom's strength tested and found wanting, but now, amid the ashes of the past, there was a glimmer of hope. He thought of the warriors who had fought bravely, their sacrifices etched into the very fabric of the land. The price of peace had been steep, but as the new day unfolded, Darion felt a stirring of resolve. The dawn of a new era was upon them, and it was his duty to lead his people into it with honor.

In Aelarion, the Sorceress Queen walked through the quiet gardens of her palace, the magic in her veins pulsing softly with the rhythm of the new day. The prophecy had loomed like a dark cloud, but now the skies were clearing. The battles were over, and with them, the weight of her personal losses seemed to lift, if only slightly. The dawn brought with it a chance to rebuild, to heal the old wounds with new hope. Lady Seraphine, ever by her side, shared in these moments of quiet reflection. They had faced shadows together, and now, they stood on the brink of a future where light could once again flourish.

King Eldric of Eryndor, his mind ever calculating, walked the deck of his mighty navy, now anchored in peaceful waters. The dawn's light shimmered off the waves, a symbol of the new peace they sought to uphold. His heart was lighter than it had been in years, but the path to this peace was lined with both hope and uncertainty. The forbidden love that had once haunted him seemed a distant memory now, replaced by the pressing need to ensure that the unity they had fought for would endure. The sea, once a battleground, now promised prosperity and calm. The dawn of a new era meant that Eldric had to steer his kingdom through these uncharted waters of peace, guiding them with the same skill that had once served him in times of conflict.

King Roderic of Tharic, though young and untested, found himself standing amidst the ruins of his kingdom's defenses, now beginning to be rebuilt. The artisans and workers toiled tirelessly as the first light of dawn touched their weary faces. Roderic saw the determination in their eyes, a reflection of his own resolve. The resources of Tharic had fueled the fight, but now, they would be the foundation for renewal. The dawn brought with it a sense of promise, a chance to transform the kingdom's fortunes and restore what had been lost. The young king was ready to embrace this challenge, to lead his people from the shadows of war into the light of peace.

In Nocturne, Lord Malakar stood in his darkened chambers, the dawn's light seeping through the heavy curtains. His thoughts were as murky as the shadows that had once veiled his realm. The price of peace was not as clear to him as it was to the others. His motives, hidden behind a mask of allegiance, still held their own secrets. As the sun rose, Malakar pondered the role he would play in this new world. His dark forces had fought alongside the allies, but the true nature of his plans remained a mystery. The dawn did not offer him clarity but rather a moment to reflect on the complex path that lay ahead.

The leaders gathered in the great hall of the allied stronghold, a place where the echoes of war had once filled the air. Now, it was a place of reflection and planning for the future. The assembly was a blend of old and new, of scars and hopes. The rulers, their faces lined with the marks of their battles, looked toward the future with a mix of caution and optimism. The dawn had brought them to this moment, but what came next was in their hands.

King Darion spoke first, his voice steady and commanding. He acknowledged the cost of their victory and the price of peace. His words were a reminder of the sacrifices made and the promises yet to be fulfilled. The dawn of a new era demanded more than just the end of conflict; it required the building of trust and the forging of new bonds.

The Sorceress Queen followed, her voice carrying the weight of both wisdom and sorrow. She spoke of the need to heal the old wounds and to embrace the light of the new day. Her words were a call to unity, a plea for the kingdoms to come together not just in name but in spirit. The magic that had once protected them now had a role in guiding them toward a future where peace could flourish.

King Eldric, with his characteristic calm, spoke of the challenges ahead. He urged his fellow rulers to navigate the delicate balance of power and trust. The dawn brought new opportunities, but also new challenges. Eldric's message was one of cautious optimism, a reminder that the path to lasting peace was fraught with difficulties but also full of potential.

King Roderic, with youthful enthusiasm, spoke of rebuilding and renewal. His vision was one of hope, a promise that the resources and strength of Tharic would be used to build a brighter future. The dawn had awakened a new determination within him, a drive to restore his kingdom to its former glory and beyond.

And Lord Malakar, ever enigmatic, observed in silence. His presence was a reminder of the complexities that still lay ahead. The dawn did not reveal his true intentions, but it marked the beginning of a new chapter in the intricate dance of alliances and power.

As the meeting concluded, the rulers parted ways with a sense of shared purpose. The dawn had brought them to this moment of reflection and planning. The future was unwritten, but the steps they took now would shape the world they hoped to build. The price of peace had been high, and the road ahead was uncertain, but as the sun rose on this new day, the leaders of the allied kingdoms faced the challenges with renewed hope and determination. The dawn was not just the start of a new day but the beginning of a new era, where unity and trust would guide them toward a brighter future.

Don't miss out!

Visit the website below and you can sign up to receive emails whenever Calvin Garner publishes a new book. There's no charge and no obligation.

https://books2read.com/r/B-A-MYSDB-YMKGF

BOOKS 2 READ

Connecting independent readers to independent writers.